IN SEARCH
OF GEDO

ISBN #0-9648299-0-8

Simu Productions, Inc.
P.O. Box 6045
Minneapolis, MN 55406

"A writer is the inspiration of other writers"

Simu

IN SEARCH OF GEDO

Isaura-Maria Simu

*This Book is Dedicated
to Humanity*

PREFACE

*T*he Subject of this book is concerned with the art of becoming better.

There will be occasions in which we, as human beings, lose ourselves in matters of materialistic existence, in which we need to call upon God's presence to help us.

We need to begin searching for his Divine Light. This will be the only way that we can assure for ourselves the salvation of our souls.

It is hoped that the content of this book might be a guide to help you seek that Light....as it has been for me.

INTRODUCTION

We speak here of the coming of a New Generation of Souls. This can be called a New Age.

Human conditions are related to human behaviors, and God's Eternal Love is within reach of us all.

The condition of the soul, no matter where we are, is important above all else.

Our common sense of humanity must be based on respect, love and tolerance. For what we are today, the life of tomorrow will be the result.

CONTENTS

Contents (continuation)

Contents (continuation)

Page

*T*he twelve illustrations and the front cover in this volume are original drawings by the author based on her own dreams.

Chapter 1

On "Being Different"

*T*his book begins with the intention of people to be different. By "different", I mean the intention of a person to make changes, to become better, to learn better to love and be loved by others. Seeking God's power is the task of our lives, in which we will find the path of our hopes.

Through our hopes we can attain the relaxing peace of our minds, and the courage necessary for the journey. Conscious mind is the gift of the Creator to us. If we seek to realize truth, if we respect and love ourselves, we can say that we are growing in our awareness and in our conscious mind.

The returning of the souls, life after life, indicates to us the importance of this awareness.

When in our minds we can conceive truth, we can say that we have achieved the triumph of the Love of God. It is a pity how many people do not realize this.

The state of consciousness of every human being depends on the realization of the continuation of life. It is a matter of understanding and realization.

What we wish to be appears as a contradiction in our own lives. Understanding this contradiction can clarify our mission

3

towards others. At the beginning of creation, man and woman were conditioned to live their external life in total communion with nature, in the unity of soul and body.

God's will shall again come from the result of this communion. *For what we are, we will be.*

Chapter 2

On Seeking Ourselves Through Spiritual Life

Seeking ourselves in this life of contradictions is a hard task, for which we have to renounce some of life's pleasures.

The continuation of God's task lies in the renunciation of desires. The awakening of the spiritual life through conscious mind is a very profound task in our lives. It is a miracle when we can assure ourselves of this task. The substance which activates the soul is the Light of God.

Our mind will record the successes of daily life and practice. This will be necessary to achieve the salvation of the soul.

There is a symbolism in all religions that connects us with the Love of God. It is the guide that helps us tell right from wrong actions. It is the learning process that determines our way forward. Our interaction with others is a matter of the learning process.

The superconscious mind exists in the relinquishing of certain desires. It will lead us to follow certain positive ways of action. Similarly, when we allow our soul to decay, our body responds. It is obvious then that something is going wrong within us. If we let our body suffer through spiritual starvation, we allow illness to take hold of it.

We have to stop this process in a very concrete way. We owe this precious gift of life to our Creator. We have the power to survive this illness. Some people reach this imbalance through certain conditions in their lives. We have the power to overcome this situation.

We actually consent to allow this behavior to destroy what is good, when we do this, it is a fact that we permit a lethargic way of life to take us over. Consciousness will bring forth what we already have in our souls.

When we detect the wrongness of this behavior, then it is truly time for change. We must determine what we really want. It is our choice. Can we be sure, then, what will make us happy? It is a question that our subconscious mind has to respond to. Take courage to make the decision, it will be a big step to make.

It is a moment of eternal contact with God. He is the mediator of all our decisions. He will seek the best, because He is Love.

Can we accept His decision?

When we are attuned with His Infinite Grace, how can we deny His protection? How can we say that He is not with us? Seeking this connection, our efforts will be rewarded.

8

"Seeing is believing". You can apply this principle to your own efforts.

Chapter 3

On Choosing the Healing Process

*T*o choose the healing process, we have to begin by working with the negativity in our subconscious mind. For this we need to prepare ourselves by a process of meditation. It is obvious that this preparation will involve much dedication and learning. We have to establish a basic rule: to desire contact with God above all else. We have to purify our bodies with the clear desire to receive His communion.

This desire will work upon us as a process of total purification. This process of learning has to be taken step by step. Can we agree with God to make these changes?

Every contact with the Lord is rewarded. Each moment of our lives is counted for Him. It is a kind desire from Him to help us to find Him.

The method for connecting available to us is the daily meditation. Through it we will receive what we need.

Body-mind working together will be the key to the connection with God. We must set a rule of self-discipline to begin the meditation practice. Our mind must be aware and ready to work into this. Our body and mind must desire this as part of our new person who is going to grow. It is necessary to draw this energy into ourselves, to want to accept it no matter what circumstances, dreams, desires, or distractions appear to stop this energy from coming through us. We have to consider His desire as part of our own desire. It will be part of His connection with us.

When we have this connection we will feel His Love and understanding toward others. The setting for the meditation can be anywhere. What is important is the peace and quietness of mind. It is necessary to surround yourself with God's Light.

The confirmation of His desire will be rewarded with His Eternal Love. It will be the most beautiful prize ever received, to be surrounded by His Eternal Light. His Eternal Love will be your protection. It is the most beautiful feeling you can ever experience in life on earth. It is the concentration of life and love together. Your will, will be His will.

Working in unison means the focusing of body-mind on God's Eternal Love. It is the process of understanding. It is God's work. Our conscious mind will rebel, not allowing us to complete the task. It will create something to distract us, to stop us from growing. It will be like a battle between enemies. This is why our desire for receiving the changes must be very powerful.

The games of the conscious mind will

bind us to a degree of low karma. The peace that arises from surrounding ourselves with God's Light will lift the karma. The sensation of this lifting will be felt in the body. The body will become available for love and understanding. The body will react with a sensation of happiness and joy. The body will react against illness. The body will be thankful. This is God's Eternal Love.

Fears will leave the mind and be replaced by sensation of freedom. The senses will be awakened to continuing this contact. They can be developed to a very deep level. They will tell of the beauty that surrounds you. The senses will tell of the necessity to lead a simple life style. They will tell you about self-control and the need for balance. They will show you the necessary awareness to stop the excesses of abusing material things here on earth. Perception is the key to self-control.

It is important that we increase this awareness with daily meditation. This will be the main tool available to help us attune ourselves to God's Eternal Love.

We have to understand that the continuation of negative behavior can become a matter of survival. It can become a matter of the self-decadency of our whole soul and body. It is very important that we continue our process of self-realization.

Regardless of all the problems that life reserves for us, we have to continue this process. It will be the purification of all that exists in our mind-body. It is God's will that we accomplish what we began. Fear will be our main enemy, subtracting from the good intention of our heart. The consequence will be our lethargy of mind. Life will continue in the same direction we are going. Life cannot be changed by itself. Certain conditions can help us to change the old pattern, but it is our responsibility to begin the change.

The conscious mind is an important part of this change. By projecting an image of change and new life, messages will be sent to our subconscious mind that will take us to the positive path. It is a pity when these connections are not a matter of awareness. Can we supply the body-mind with the energy-power these changes require?

Something will tell us to stop, but awareness will tell us to go on. What I have expressed will sound contradictory, but these are the things that we run into in everyday life, contradictions that make no sense but we live them anyway. These are the contradictions that society obligates us to follow. We call them customs.

The sequence of these habits will produce a state of absence or non-contact with our inner self. We may continue on this path that we feel makes us comfortable, even though we know the sense of guilt, unhappiness, and disappointment in our hearts. Yet changing our life can be rewarded with the infinite peace and harmony of God's Eternal Love.

Chapter 4

On Negative Behavior as Self-decadency of Our Soul

Searching for truth can lead us to changes we may not feel ready to make. Is like searching for something that we do not know. That is why our desire to find it has to be strong. *"Seeing is believing."*

There was a man who did not believe in anything, but asked God for a proof of His existence. God told him to look at himself, and in that he would find truth.

How can man have doubts about his own creation?

How can man ask God for proof when he cannot see himself as one of His creations?

Since his creation, man in his continuing search for God's Love has forgotten that he is part of God, that if he opens his eyes fully, he will find Him in his own heart. God's infinite Love will not ask for proof from man by doubting His own worth. This is a reaction due to man's own lack of belief.

Conditions will make man deny himself in front of God. It is this misfortune that plagues man now. His own concerns are more important to him than God's existence. It will be a long way to the point of finding God's Love if he doesn't change his attitude toward himself. Creation was made for man's joy.

Why does his attitude threaten to destroy this? Conditions are created by man, why does he follow them with closed eyes and deny God's existence?.

Man says: "I will find Him someday." But he doesn't want to know that God already has found him.

The molecules of man's body form a powerful cord to connect him with God. This cord will keep him close to His infinite way of Love.

The Flow

Chapter 5

On Searching for the Truth

As part of our learning process, there is a consequent realization. Every day we will see the rewarding of our efforts. Every day we will see the connections, how this process makes us feel and perceive God's Eternal Love.

Some will think: But how can I get there? I will tell you that effort is necessary to get things. It is a matter of giving and receiving.

We can just imagine the little bird who is crossing in the sky. He is making an effort in moving his wings, and the rest is done by nature. If we make the effort to move our desires to reach God, it will be the most beautiful move on our part. Nature can help us learn how to act. Her perfection tells us of the connection with God.

Why don't we want to be part of this perfection? Regardless of our imperfections we are part of Her, and God wants us to be perfect like all His creations. But how can I be perfect when I am living in a world where imperfection is everywhere caused by mankind? If we start with the perfection in ourselves, it will lead us to more perfection, if we stop our growing just because other people's imperfections are affecting us, this leads us to disadvantage. Since we are God's creation, our pattern should be His creation. *"For what we are we shall receive."*

Chapter 6

On Our Actions

When our actions are controlled by impulse, we can dissolve this negativity with love. When our actions are controlled by karma, we have to redeem ourselves through understanding.

If we disregard the first point, we disregard our self-worth and become victims of desperation and disappointment. If we disregard the second point, we also contribute to our own unhappiness. If we look within, we will discover that the problem lies simply in the demands of the conscious mind.

It is a matter of fact that we all have the key to open the door that will take us to Divine contact with God. We can open this door any time we want, but we allow our indecision and fears to take us over. We may feel it is easier to hold on to this attitude, even when we see that our heart is suffering.

Why don't we do something about our behavior? Because at the moment that we are about to make a decision to stop this negative behavior, our conscious mind controls our impulses and the conscious mind is conditioned to earthly life. We seek help from it, but by itself it will bring no answers. Allowing these problems to take possession of us, we will be pushed to the border of desperation. Desperation will lead us to the nightmare of loneliness and disappointment. We must stop without hesitation. *Seeing is believing.*

> *There was once a man who respected himself, then he was tempted by conditions he thought would offer a better and more exciting life, and he sacrificed his purity and happiness to get it, but the prize that thought he was going to receive, he was to pay back with his own health.*
> *He thought: "I am so clever that I will keep everything under control, so that all this will not affect me". Time passed and now the man can see the consequences of this action, he is a slave of all his desires and he has no power to reject them. Seeing is believing.*

Can we continue living under these conditions? No. We cannot let them take us over. For we are the Divine Children of God. For Him we are His creation, how can we abandon Him, how can we deny Him, how can we exchange Him for all the materialistic things that have no price or volume?

Look to His eyes and we will find them full of love and compassion. Look in his heart and we will find strength and power. He will never abandon us. He will never reject us. He is always there, waiting to be found.

Can we make the effort and seek Him? He will take our hand and guide us to His Infinite Love. He will show us the most beautiful paradise that is in His heart. He will say to us: You are my beloved children, please come to me. He will have tears in His eyes to redeem our faults. He will love us for ever and ever in His unchanging Love.

Chapter 7

On Being Conditioned to Materialistic Life

*B*eing conditioned to a materialistic life style can make us centered on physical pleasures. Our life can turn into a nightmare of persecutors and victims. *For what we are we shall receive.*

Blaming ourselves for these matters will not help us, for is the continuing mistakes from man that keeps him away from God.

It is a man's decision to make this change, for he is both the creator and the victim of that nightmare. When we make that decision, things will begin to change, but we have to keep ourselves from falling again into the same mistake.

Strength is very important in this decision. We will discover that this strength will come from our daily meditation and practice. It will come from our love of God that is in our hearts and we have awakened.

Let us say that we continue on the old path of suffering simply because we are familiar with it. It is the path we know. This decision can lead us into a long period of physical suffering. It can lead us to poor health. It can lead us to think we need to purify our mind and body as separate tasks, when we can do everything at once by simply purifying one part of ourselves, the soul.

It is amazing what a human being can do if he is willing to. Premonitions of what is right and wrong come from our behavior, as I have said before. Premonitions of what is healthy and unhealthy will come from our body. When the body stars falling apart, it is time for major change. Body-mind are deeply connected. Body-mind-God are connected to help us to stop the self-destruction towards which man is heading. Can we act to stop this destruction?

There was a man once that did not want to live. He would say every day in his prayers: Please God take me with you, since I can no longer live in this world. God answered him, telling him of the necessity to direct his prayers upon himself. Then the man said: "But you are God, how I can send these prayers to myself?" To that God answered: "Look in the mirror and you will find the God that is within you. He will listen carefully and He will help you to find the love that you are seeking."

Man is a projection of God's image. Can man not see it in this way? Everyday life conditions man to forget who he is. Can we condition ourselves to find God? *Seeing is believing.*

Spirituality

Chapter 8

On Love for Ourselves

*O*ur demonstration of love for ourselves involves a determination to become better. When we don't do this we put ourselves down.

Why do we think that we don't deserve love? It is because we don't know what love means. Love, what a beautiful word!

Can we imagine living in a world where everything is under the karma of love? Can we imagine living in total harmony with ourselves and others? Can we imagine how our eyes filled with love will look at others people's eyes?

The act of loving is a consequence of receiving. But why don't we take this action? Simply because our fear of losing ourselves in the other person doesn't let us do it. What does loosing ourselves in others mean? It means that in giving ourselves to others we are afraid of losing ourselves. We don't believe that giving is receiving. We have doubt about the Divine nature of sharing. We want to keep everything for ourselves, including love. It is this a consequence of our behavior? Yes, if we deny to others what we have, we are denying to ourselves the right to be happy.

Why are we so attached to these things?

Because we think about our right to posses
things, without thinking that all worldly
possessions cannot be exchanged for anything
that will compare with God's Eternal Love. It
is a matter of fact that He will be the only
one that can make us happy. *Seeing is
believing.*

> *There was a time when a group of
> men were living together in a
> community. One man got sick and
> wanted help from the others.
> Nobody came to his room. He
> decided to get up and see what
> the others were doing. When he
> reached the next room, he saw the
> rest of the group gathered,
> conversing. He said to them: "Do
> you not worry about your fellow
> brother that is sick?" The group
> answered him: "We do not worry
> about you, for you are not sick in
> your soul, just in your body."*

It is easy to understand that our soul
needs more care that our bodies. Why do we
abandon the care of our souls? Is it just
because we don't see it?

Our soul is the Divine Gift from God.
The consequences of this abandonment are
devastating. Laziness, impurity and decadency

of our moral life are the result. Why don't we stop this? Because we think that it will take too much of our precious time to take care of our soul.

We think that nothing that our eyes cannot see or our hands cannot touch has substance. Since we don't know the feeling of peace and happiness in our mind and heart, we ignore this feeling in exchange for materialistic things. But it is possible to attain a feeling of happiness and self-satisfaction that we will not want to lose, but to preserve for ever and ever. It is simply the feeling of love and being loved.

Chapter 9

On Perceptions

*P*erceptions are a very important part of our experience. We need to listen to them very carefully. They are the awakening part in us. When proper perceptions are awakened, we have the opportunity to follow a path of understanding ourselves.

How can we feel that our perceptions are opening? When we know that we can control our feelings, when we know right from wrong, when we know that our body is speaking to us.

When we ignore the awakening of our perceptions, we ignore ourselves. How can we ignore ourselves? Simply, when we forget about our soul-body-God.

Can we do something about this? Yes, we can start healing this problem with daily meditation. Our constant contact with God will help us to be in contact with ourselves. It is truth. Why, then, do we insist on losing ourselves in the race for materialistic things? Because we have no time for God's things, we feel no worth in ourselves, and we are careless with our soul.

The conditions that man has set up for himself here on earth are taking him away from God, and he doesn't want to know it. It is a shame that man denies this truth in front of himself. *Seeing is believing.*

> *There was a man once, who kept saying to himself: "I am nobody, I have no worth in front of my family and friends. I am good for nothing. Why do I have to be here in this world where nothing is important to me and I am not important to anybody?"*
> *When he was deeply immersed in his negative thoughts, something appeared in front of him. He was afraid of this apparition, but then he listened to a voice which told him: "How can you say these words to yourself? Don't you see how much I love you? Don't you see that I died on the cross because I love you?"*
> *The man, after hearing these words, never again felt sorry for himself.*

How can we deny God's presence when He is with us at all times? Awakening these perceptions is a very important task for humankind, for we are part of the whole of creation, God's creation.

We cannot continue living in the world of self-destruction. We cannot continue seeing ourselves as   miserable creatures in this Universe. If we continue accepting these thoughts as a part of our daily life, without correcting them, we will remain in the same place, perceiving unhappiness over and over.

Correcting our mistakes will give us satisfaction and results that are positive. Our feelings will reflect our triumphs.

Chapter 10

On Imbalances in the Physical Life

*T*here are occasions when man is troubled by things not related to the spiritual path, one could say illnesses, imbalances in the physical life. This situation is due to the malfunction of certain glands that control the nervous system.

The process to follow in resolving these types of imbalances involves the total rest of the body, possibly with the use of medications or various kinds of therapy. The person's spiritual life is reduced in this situation, since the person may no longer be in control of his feelings. The person may actually not be totally responsible for his actions at such a time. We cannot demand from this person full responsibility for his life because he cannot respond fully at that time.

How can we spiritually help this person who is suffering from such a physical imbalance? Simply with the patience that God has used to help us find ourselves, to find love and understanding.

There was a man once who attempted to commit suicide. He had found that there was something wrong in his behavior. Thinking that he did not want to

57

be a burden to his family, he decided to end his life. When he was ready to die, Jesus came to him and, holding his hands, He told him: "My beloved child, do not feel guilty, it is not your fault that certain mechanisms of the body are not working well for you. Life is precious, and not to be ended because of this. Why don't you turn your eyes to our Creator and let Him take care of you."

How we take care of our physical body speaks to our appreciation of ourselves. Why can't we do the same with our soul?

We shower our bodies almost every day, we put on perfumes and nice clothes to show others how proud we are of our bodies, but often we don't do the same with our soul.

Our soul needs to wear the most expensive perfume, the perfume of love, and the most expensive garment, the garment of faith. Can we spend more time to dress our soul? It takes more time to dress our body than our soul. Dressing our body, we will receive the admiration of our fellow man. Dressing our soul, we will receive the admiration of God's Love.

Chapter 11

On Obstacles that Prevent Our Growth

*T*he obstacles that prevent our growth come from guilt and from the physical senses. Why can't we develop immunity against these? Because of our slavery to getting everything in an easy way. This is why our spirit of sacrifice is dead. We don't want to give anything for nothing. It is the quality of perception and openness that allows us to give and receive.

Self-sacrifice for our own good seems even worse to us because we don't expect anything from ourselves, because our love for ourselves is so poor that we think we don't deserve anything good. For this reason we try to supply our spiritual necessities with material things, thinking that this will fill us up. We protect ourselves from sacrifice.

Caring and concern about ourselves comes from the desire to be happy. Detachment from the materialistic life can bring us rewards of self-contentment, knowledge, love, understanding, tolerance and beauty in life.

There was a man once who accumulated all the money he could from his business, thinking that all this abundance would make his life happy and secure. One day a poor man came to his door and asked him for help, for food or money to buy it. He looked at the man and said: "Why are you in this situation of poverty? Why didn't you think about yourself as I did, when good times were around you? Don't you see the mistake you have made in not preventing this poverty that you are suffering now?"

The poor man looked at him and answered: "Questions, questions, questions. All regarding material things! God our Father, He will not question us when we ask Him for forgiveness, help and understanding. He will simply look at us and love us, just the way we appear to Him. This is the magnificence of His Eternal Love."

Why don't we begin our change? Because personal matters stop our growth. We don't want to be less than others. At any moment we can realize that we are part of God, and for Him we are all the same. Why don't we realize the fact we are all equal before God's eyes?

It seems to us that it is a high price to pay. We will not accept it, because this sacrifice will take us to a renunciation of our power over other human beings. We cannot accept being treated all in the same way, as humans, not according to color or money or titles or positions.

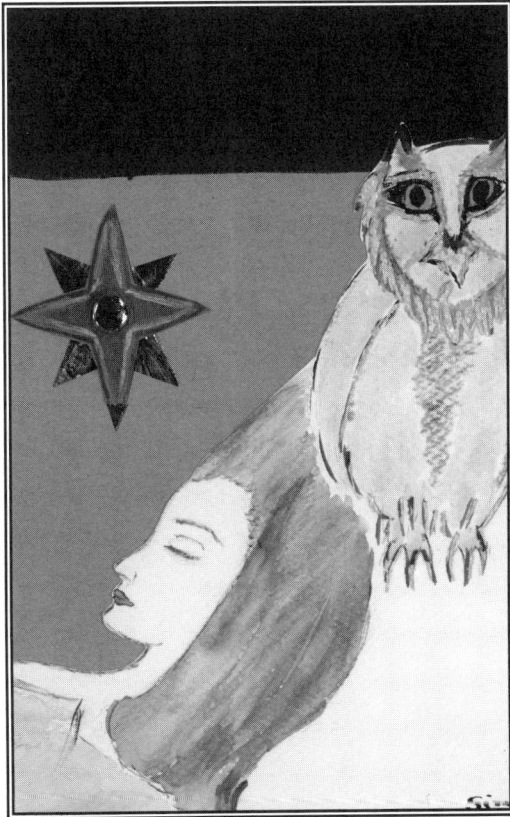

Wisdom

*Don't be afraid, I am not going
to hurt you*

Chapter 12

On Feeling
Sorry for Ourselves

*I*n our lives we are predisposed to feel inadequate for many reasons. We always look for any excuse to feel sorry for ourselves. We continue our daily life as usual, then we take the consequences of this behavior as punishment. We believe that we are here in this world to suffer the consequences of our existence. In fact, we are here to testify to our karma, to make the necessary growth, to return or receive from others what we have done to others before.

Can we recognize these actions when we are close to them? When we approach these actions, we will sense the knowledge of something that our mind cannot recall. It is a matter of recognizing our mistakes from the past. Being aware of these feelings is very important, for it affects what happens to our karma. *For what we are we shall receive.*

There was a man once who ignored his karma. One day he saw a man who recognized him at first glance. He denied knowing the man, but the other man insisted that there was a connection between the two of them. When he was about to deny these feelings one more time, the other man spoke: "What will this life be if we don't take care of our debts to others? We will never have rest from our karma if we don't pay our past debts."

Karma involves the consequences of our actions. Why are we afraid to face these consequences? Taking care of ourselves will help us grow. Denying these feelings will just stop our changing of old habits.

The life performance is like a theater, we act for others and forget to act first for ourselves. Why have we to wear a mask just to meet other's expectations? Because we are afraid of other people's objections. We think that our mission in life is to make other people happy and to forget our own happiness.

We cannot deny our fears of not being accepted by others. These fears keep us from finding happiness in ourselves. If we look at ourselves in our mirror, we will discover the conflicted life that we are living. It will be reflected in our own faces, behavior and feelings. Why don't we stop these actions, when we see clearly they are affecting our karma?

Sending a message to our subconscious mind will help us stop this behavior. Giving importance to ourselves will help us stop this behavior. Loving and accepting ourselves the way we are, will help our self to grow. *For what we are we shall receive.*

Chapter 13

On Making Decisions

*T*he circumstances man has to deal with sometimes make him feel incompetent in making his own decisions. The decision to be different, to make a better life, will be based on the desire for great change.

Why major change? Because the solution to our sorrows and problems has to be carved out in that way. If we center ourselves in materialistic living, how can we expect a solution to come to us? Just pretending to have a happy life without problems will take us nowhere.

Truth is a matter of being lifted from this life of materialism. Why is it so difficult for most of us to be happy? Because of our continuous desire to have more possessions.

We must control our desire to satisfy ourselves only with body pleasures. We must control ourselves from using our power over others. We must control ourselves from being dominated by the sadness and sorrow of having less material things.

Thinking in this way will help us to find the peace and happiness that we are looking for. Why are we so unhappy when things don't come at the moment we want them? Because we base our life on schedules and desires. When something that we ask for doesn't come along at the moment we expect it, we fail to recognize that our dreams and desires have not been satisfied because our attitude was negative.

Can we do something about this? Yes, with daily meditation our mind will be released from these forces of desire. We will realize that patience is one of the greatest efforts that man must achieve in finding peace. Why don't we make things easier for ourselves and others? *Seeing is believing.*

The consequences that come from our actions are a matter that requires understanding. *For what we are we shall receive.*

> *There was a man once who expected a large number of things to come to his house. He was ashamed in front of his family when all the promises he had made to them were not fulfilled at the right moment or time he had promised. He came to his family to explain why the things didn't arrive. Before he started talking, his wife intervened and said: Why worry about the things that didn't arrive, when we have something that has no price in this world, which is the love that we feel for*

each other?. We need to appreciate what is already in our hands and not suffer for what is not here yet.

Chapter 14

On Denying God's Eternal Love

Suppose that we deny God's Eternal Love in order to justify our faults and mistakes. Why then do we feel so disappointed when we turn our faces and look upon ourselves? When we cannot accept truth coming from within ourselves, it is because we are denying this reality.

Why is it that we alone cannot stop this suffering? Only if we seek God's presence in our hearts can we stop it. Denying this reality is denying to ourselves the right to be happy. Can we accelerate this desire to be happy? Yes. Simply through the love for ourselves that comes from God's presence.

Contact with the state of grace with God will project us to infinite joy. It will take us to the paradise that is in His heart. We will never, never be frightened, abandoned or lonely again. Lack of love and understanding for ourselves will never, never be again. The epidemic illness of drugs and sex comes from the lack of love and understanding of ourselves.

This race toward destruction that man is going through is simply a lack of self-realization. Seeking what we are in drugs is denying to ourselves what comes from God's Eternal Love. It is casting ourselves to the edge of our own extinction.

Why don't we make the effort to stop this degradation? Because we have no interest in keeping ourselves alive. *Seeing is believing.* What is it that makes us feel guilty for being in this world? What is it that makes us believe that we don't deserve to be happy? What is it that makes us think that destroying ourselves is the fastest way to get to the end of our problems?

Education and information are important tools to clarify areas of man's ignorance. It is a matter of the desire for knowledge. When we ignore this desire, we are pushing ourselves further into darkness. Why? Because we think it is better to know nothing than to know everything.

> *There was a man once who denied the presence of God in his reflections. When he became sick with a strange type of illness, then he came seeking God's Love and Compassion to heal him. When he was near death his conscious mind said: "Please God, forgive me for what I have done to myself in this life, for denying your beautiful presence."*

God in His compassion liberates the one

who seeks it, lifting the heavy weight of guilt. His Divine presence in our hearts, His infinite compassion and love, has no limitations. Sometimes we deny His compassion to ourselves, ignoring His presence, but it will not take too long to realize the mistakes that we have made. *Seeing is believing.*

If we don't stop ourselves from self-destruction, we are denying God's Eternal Love. How closely is our reality related to our own happiness?

When our body doesn't respond to our desire to change our old habits, we should recognize that our senses are controlling our minds. If our senses are out of control, they will bring confusion to us. We will attack our body as our enemy. We will harm our body on this path of deterioration.

In our past lives we have been doing similar things, creating the same situations in response to our body's desires. We will continue the path of destruction over and over without solution. We will come back to this world life after life without learning our mission. We accept this self-determination as a natural part of our daily life, we make no efforts to change it or to make things better for ourselves. We don't want to change.

What is it that keeps us from getting better? It is simply the lack of love for ourselves, the conscious mind keeping us apart from our subconscious. We retard our growth to satisfy the conscious mind. We let things take us over and stop the positive changes from coming.

The compatibility that we create between God and ourselves will help us break out of this circle. It is a matter of friendship, of contact, of helping. The consequences we harvest of this beautiful friendship will be the love and acceptance of ourselves and others.

LOOK AT THE SKIES AND LEARN, LOOK AT NATURE AND LEARN, LOOK AT THE GOOD SOULS AND LEARN. Everything that is in contact with the Creator works well. Everything that is in contact with God's Eternal Love, receives. Everything touching His power will work like Him.

Chapter 15

On Living in the Darkness

*F*ollowing the ways we set for ourselves here on earth, we will continue living in darkness. Correcting them in time will take us to the light. Living in the darkness is like walking blind on busy streets without a cane.

Why does man so insist on walking without help? Because his self-assurance tells him not to call for help, not to see the light, not to show his spiritual needs to anybody. Too much self-assurance is too much pride and such pride is arrogant. We cannot deny God's presence as part of us, we cannot say, "I am the powerful and perfect one of God's creation here on earth". Sometimes we prefer not to realize what we are doing to ourselves. Pride will lead us nowhere.

Since we are creatures of God, we cannot cut ourselves off from the necessity of being in contact with Him. *For what we are we shall receive.* Conditions limit us to thinking that we can do everything for ourselves. We can create things for ourselves, we can destroy things for ourselves. But we cannot continue living for ourselves if we don't have contact with God. It is a matter of self-realization, with Divine help.

If our pride allows us to ignore God's Eternal Love, if our pride allows us to ignore

His presence, we will be walking without developing our senses, without protecting ourselves from danger. It is a matter of recognition, to be thankful to our Creator by simply following the direction He wishes to guide us.

Why is it that we don't want to know about it? Because we are afraid that He will obligate us to renounce the attachments that we have developed to material things.

Can we do something about this? Yes. We can work within ourselves to find a way of pleasing Him. We can seek things that help us to get in touch with Him. Self-discipline will direct us to His hands.

Why is it that we are so reluctant to follow the path that will take us to His Eternal Love?, why is it that we fail to understand that it is impossible to keep walking or doing everything by ourselves without His help?

We are suffering the consequences of these actions right now. Loneliness, love starvation, hate and powerlessness. Even suffering these consequences, we continue living the way we are, and we don't choose to do anything about it.

Consistency is necessary to find the strength for this kind of action. We need to develop self-discipline. We need to have the desire to be ourselves part of God's creation.

It is necessary to see and feel His Love in everything, in every act, in every moment of our lives. We cannot continue denying this truth, we cannot continue denying the necessity of being with Him.

Creating love in our hearts will help us to continue walking on the path of fulfillment. It will help us to see and feel the meaning of happiness and self-realization. It will help us connect ourselves with our inner God. It will help us to be kind and loving to our fellow brother, to trust and be trustful, to choose what is best for ourselves and others, to keep our hearts away from hate and misunderstanding, to determine what is good or not, to see reality carefully, giving us the opportunity to make good decisions, showing us that we and God are one in this world created by Him. It will help us see that the world has been created to be an enjoyable place to live, and that we have the right to live in this Paradise created by God for humankind.

When we understand these gifts coming from our Creator, then we will know what happiness means.

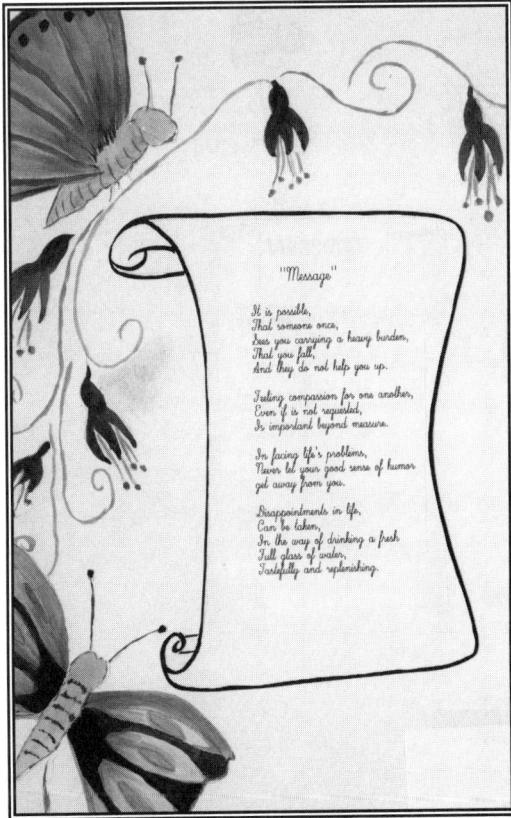

"Message"

It is possible,
That someone once,
Sees you carrying a heavy burden,
That you fall,
And they do not help you up.

Feeling compassion for one another,
Even if is not requested,
Is important beyond measure.

In facing life's problems,
Never let your good sense of humor
get away from you.

Disappointments in life,
Can be taken,
In the way of drinking a fresh
Full glass of water,
Tastefully and replenishing.

The Message

"Message"

It is possible,
That someone once,
Sees you carrying a heavy burden,
That you fall,
And they do not help you up.

Feeling compassion for one another,
Even if is not requested,
Is important beyond measure.

In facing life's problems,
Never let your good sense of humor
get away from you.

Disappointments in life,
Can be taken,
In the way of drinking a fresh
Full glass of water,
Tastefully and replenishing.

Chapter 16

On Living in Ignorance

We see that our bodies have become an empty carcass, and we insist on living in ignorance because we don't know how to handle the things that God has created for us. We deny that our lives are empty because we say there is no future or past for us, just the present. How little we know about ourselves, that we don't try to go further!

The quality of life is the quality of our karma, we cannot deny this. When we see that the life that we are living right now is not what we expect, then we put ourselves down. We cannot believe that this quality of life that we are living is what we really want. Acknowledging what we are doing wrong to ourselves helps us to get off the false path that we are following.

Why is it so difficult for human beings to recognize mistakes? Because is difficult to face them, to admit to our proud-self that we are suffering because of our own errors.

Making the right connection with our Creator will help us to move ahead with our desire for change. He just wants us to live a peaceful and happy life. He just wants the best for us. He just wants us, His children, to feel the most precious and beautiful of feelings, the feeling of love.

Can we realize all these changes? Yes, we can!, when we realize His desire for us to be different, then we begin to realize these changes. We can agree with what He is offering us, and see what our stubborn attitude brings to us. It is a matter of decision.

When we see our body decay because we are careless about these matters, then we realize how important it is to live in His grace, to follow His direction, to live in a simple way, to let things be and not be possessed by things.

It is a matter of fact that the world we are living in right now is not a helpful place to realize these changes. But if we have already in our heart the desire to be different, it will not take a special place or a long time to attain them.

The purity of our hearts will take us to the right place. That is why it is so important to be good of heart, humble and gentle to ourselves and others. This is the beginning of our changes.

"The humble will be the blessed ones because the Kingdom of God will be for them."

We don't accept being humble because of our fears that we are going to be taken advantage of by others. God's Eternal Love will take care of this. He will not leave His children abandoned to be used by others. He will see that the others pay their debt for what they do to His beloved children. This is why is so important that our behavior of taking advantage of humble persons be corrected. The law of the karma is such.

"Blessed are the good of heart because for them is the Kingdom of God."

Chapter 17

On Problems and Solutions

*A*ll the problems that appear in our daily life, all have their own solution. We think that because we live under the pressure of all these problems, that our happiness is so far away that it is almost impossible to reach. Why do we let all these problems run our lives? Because we don't have the tools to cope with them. We become so sensitive to all these problems that we cannot think of anything else, just of them. If we look closely, we can see that many of these problems are caused by our own beliefs.

When we feel empty and separate from God's Eternal Love, then we need to fill ourselves with something, and that something will be these problems.

Can we do something about this? Yes, we can put ourselves in daily contact with our Creator through meditation. We can occupy our minds with helping others who need to be helped in some way. We can contemplate the beauty and perfection of Mother Nature. We can do our own simple or difficult daily tasks with love and patience, not as a punishment. It is very important that our minds are filled with positive thoughts. As a result of all these positive thoughts in our minds, we will receive rewards from God.

Can we start doing this and keep doing it? Yes, the effort that we put into this will be rewarded with peace of mind and a healthy body.

What will stop us from doing this? Laziness, irresponsibility, lack of love, physical desires. Somehow, we will manage to find a way of not doing this. Everyday there will be some excuse to ourselves. We will seek a way to avoid this responsibility to ourselves. We think avoiding it will make our life easier. It is true that it will take effort to start on the path of self-responsibility.

We say: Life is short. Why do I have to bother myself looking for more responsibilities than I already have? Situations will come up. We will feel sick, or too hot, or too cold, or too uncomfortable, or too tired, or whatever idea comes to our mind. Our mind will work against our desire to be better.

For spiritual growth we have no time. For bodily pleasures we have all the time we need. When we don't have time for spiritual growth, we are denying health to our body. It will not take us too long to realize the discrepancy we sense when our body is not responding to our wish to make it happy only with material things. It will be a matter of feeling and observing. *Seeing is believing.*

Chapter 18

On Changes

We have to realize that if it is difficult for us to see reality, it is equally difficult for us to change. One is connected to the other.

Changes don't come just by themselves.
Changes need to be accepted by us.
Changes must be programmed by us.
Changes have to be made for our own good.

We have realized that these changes can be done right now!

"THESE POSITIVE CHANGES RESULT IN POSITIVE THOUGHTS."

There is a connection between the positive part of our thoughts and the positive part of our desires. When this connection is made, action comes. The reward for this action is what the soul perceives and receives.

The reward coming from God for our actions is most beautiful, we cannot deny this. He knows what is best for His children. He knows of their needs. He knows the right time to give this reward to them. When we receive this reward, the wonder can be seen in our eyes. We can feel the reaction in our body. We can see how much time we have been wasting just trying to reward our actions by ourselves. Our own rewarding cannot be compared with His rewarding.

There was a man once who complained and complained about his miserable life. He said: "I don't understand. I am a good man. I go to church every day, I confess my sins, I go to communion every day, I am a good father, I am a good Christian. Why it is that my life has no rewards in this world?"

Following directions implanted by mankind will take you nowhere. Following the direction implanted in you by God's Eternal Love will take you directly to His heart. That will be your reward.

Man is seduced here on earth by life conditions. God's Eternal Love is unconditional. He is just there to give to whomever asks of Him.

Nature shows its connection with Him. We have only to wait for the rain, for the sunshine, or for the wind. Then Nature returns her love for Him with beauty, happiness, and perfection. We cannot deny this.

Change is very important to stop self-destruction. It is the only way to get in contact with God. *Seeing is believing.*

Searching for the truth will take us to the joy of finding it. Searching for God will take us to the joy of seeing ourselves reflected in Him. Because we are *ONE.*

Chapter 19

On Coping with Problems

*T*he feeling of being unable to cope with problems comes from our own indecision about making a new and different life. We depend so much on the suffering of our daily life, that we close our minds to all kind of positive thoughts. The negativity coming from this behavior can lead us to a resolution to end our life.

Can we do something about this? Yes. The solution has to come from within us. Nobody will help us cope with these problems. It is a matter of our responsibility to take care of ourselves. If we continue acting selfishly with our soul and body, we should think about the end we are going to have.

It is a matter of self-realization of the need to take care of ourselves. The conditions related to all these problems come from our lack of love, knowledge, and understanding of our own body system. We play games with our body, thinking that it is something that we are not going to take with us when we die. But we care for our material possessions without thinking that we are not going to take them with us when we die.

Why is it that we don't take care of our body, that we sometimes destroy it with problems, illnesses, and drugs?

Lack of knowledge of our body system leads us to think that if we harm it we can get it back again somehow. It is the lack of understanding of our own senses that makes us ignore our own body when it is calling for help. How can we deny this!

Nature is the most beautiful example of synchronization, respect, and love. The beauty coming from nature is related to the contact she has with our Creator. The beauty coming from man is related to the contact he has with God's Eternal Love. The consequences of destroying beauty fall upon man. He manages somehow to let things die because he is careless with them. It is due to a lack of love and understanding. *Seeing is believing.*

We deny this truth because it is our favorite game. Deny, deny everything. God sees all these errors that man with his problems is committing upon himself. He waits until man turns his face to Him asking for help, and then He will always be there.

When man gets tired of destroying himself, he will turn his eyes to His Creator and he will find His heart open and full of love, waiting for him. When man gets tired of being punished by his own hand, he will turn his eyes to Him and will find forgiveness and understanding of his faults.

112

I am the Way

Chapter 20

On Understanding Human Behavior

*U*ntil now we have spoken about problems and solutions. What if we speak about understanding human behavior?

Much human behavior comes from our fears and insecurities. We have been burdened with many fears since we came out from our mother's womb. We already see that the world is painful, we realize it in seeking contact with it.

Why? Because the hands that take us out of our mother's body already transmit this pain to us. When we surrender ourselves to these hands, we give away the right to be happy and free from pain. Our conscious mind will take and will record this pain for life.

Why is it that we cannot erase this pain from our minds? Because it will be part of us until we die. It is the first experience of pain we receive coming into the world. It is a fact that we will retain this impression of pain until we realize that we didn't come here to suffer or to feel guilty. We came here to redeem our karma for all that we have done to others. After we have paid for our faults, the choice to be happy or to feel guilty for the rest of our lives is in our hands. *Seeing is believing.*

The consequences of continuing on the path of this negative behavior conform to our karma. We have to realize this. When we know that we are free from our faults, we can move ahead freely.

> *There was a man once who always said to his friends: "My heart feels free of sin because my mind is at peace."*
> *One of his friends said to him one day: "How can you say that so freely when you are not ready to finish your promises here on earth?" But the man's answer was: "When I say I am free, my mind is at peace, I have a duty to myself, to love and accept myself first, showing to others in this way how wonderful it is to be here."*

Demonstrating to others how happy and accepting we are with ourselves is very important. We can help others in this way, showing them that we have conquered pain, the pain that is with us from the day we are born. It is a matter of self-realization, it is a matter of acceptance, it is a matter of growth.

Pain, how much fear we feel just thinking about it. Pain doesn't let us forget

118

things. Pain can stay with us for ever and ever if we don't do something to overcome it.

People often don't know how to conquer pain. They let it take over, because pain lets us feel sorry for ourselves, and that is the negative part of us.

We treat pain as an important ally in our daily life. We may never know how we can live our life without it. If we had the opportunity to live without pain, we would manage to seek it, because without pain we feel our life would be without meaning.

In consequence, we will create situations like the initial time of our birth, to return again to that pain.

Chapter 21

On Gaining Control of Our Conscious Mind

*I*f we look for what we have left behind, we will never get anywhere. We need to keep our minds clear for the new things to come. We cannot continue living in the darkness just because our conscious mind tells us to do so. This is why it is so important to gain control of our conscious mind and to keep it occupied.

We cannot deny that the conscious mind plays many games with us that can make us lose control of ourselves. We must be watchful of our conscious mind. *Seeing is believing.*

There was once a man who decided to separate himself from God's teachings. He thought that if he followed his conscious mind everything would be all right. One day he was doing his daily tasks when a man appeared to him and asked:

"Why are you here each day doing this tedious job, when you could be living in a palace enjoying all the good things that rich people enjoy? Why live in such poverty, when I can give you anything you want for just a few

123

things in exchange?"
The man, as a matter of curiosity,
replied: "Who are you who is
offering me all these things, and
what it is that you want in
exchange?" To which the man
answered: "Why do you ask who
I am, if in a simple thought you
should know it?"

The qualities of being a good person are always there. The problem comes when we let these qualities slip away, simply because we want to build an easy life for ourselves.

The temptations of our daily life are there always. Succumbing to these temptations brings problems, for we lack strength and security in our thoughts. This is when the temptations take us over. They will push us to put aside the good things that are in us. It is a struggle, and we need to know how to fight back. Otherwise we will succumb to them.

These temptations are not always of money, power, or sex. They are of doing bad things to others, of revenge towards people who make us feel disappointed about ourselves.

All these situations are opportunities for us to use our strength. Negative consequences come back to us from our incapacity to fight back against temptation. These temptations present themselves through opportunities to take things from others. *Seeing is believing.*

When the time comes that we begin to realize these mistakes, this will be the time for change. This will be the time for turning ourselves to our Creator. It will be the time to correct ourselves and to ask for forgiveness, not just from our Creator, but also from the people whom we have harmed. It will be the time to realize that our old ways will take us nowhere. *For what we are we shall receive.*

Chapter 22

On Life, Our Most Precious Gift

*T*he satisfactions of life come from the desire to be better. We decide how we are going to lead our life. We make the decision that can lead to destroying it. It is our own choice, we cannot deny this.

When are we going to understand that life is the most precious gift coming from our Creator to us? The sensitivity to appreciate this gift is a matter of our own choice. We cannot deny this, either.

When we decide to take our life, just because we are not content with what we are doing or with what we are, we are destroying and rejecting God's gift. This is a matter of fear, fear to live what has been given to us by God. In destroying this beautiful gift, we are rejecting Him, we are destroying His love for us, His compassion, we are denying that we are His beloved children, that He cares about us. We are denying to ourselves the right to be happy.

We cannot continue making this mistake. We cannot continue destroying what He has created. We cannot continue denying Him anymore.

There was a man once who rejected his life. He was very

unhappy, even though he was a healthy and wealthy man. Preparing to take his life, he said to himself:

"What is this life for, when I am not happy being here, even though I have everything? What is this life good for, when the person I love so much has left me without any reason?"

When He was almost ready to take his life, he heard a voice that said to him:

"My beloved child, why do you say all these things to yourself and deny me in your thoughts?"

Before we decide to do something destructive to ourselves, we must turn ourselves to our Creator, and then we will find His love and understanding. It is a matter of understanding that God's Infinite Love is waiting for us, that He has all the necessary time to help us, that He will never deny help to us.

Can we come to Him and ask for help if we need it?

Our conscious mind will say to us that to contact Him is not necessary, for we have all these material things to take care of. The conscious mind will say to us that turning ourselves to God it is wasting time for we cannot see Him or touch Him. Our conscious mind will tell us that it is an illusion to believe that He will take care of us in our hard moments, when we don't know where He is.

The one who creates us will take care of us. *Seeing is believing.*

Chapter 23

On Experience of Being Rich or Poor

*T*he experience of being poor can lead us to the point of being harmless to others. Our own actions can cause us to be happy and to live without pretentiousness.

Since this world is populated with people filled only with the desire to possess material things, the poor need to be here to show others the quality of being humble and good of heart. They show others that ambition for possessions will not bring them to the place of love and understanding.

The concern that some people show over lacking material things will make them unhappy. Worrying about this will take them to the same point as the rich who have too much. Being simple, living simply, and accepting the simplicity coming from our Creator is what will make us happy. *For what we are we shall receive.*

There are occasions when we become confused, thinking about why some people get much and others get nothing.

We need to accept being born in this world in the way that God wants us to be. It is the alternative to choose the good or the bad that He gives to us. It is His own decision that we come to this world with a great deal or with nothing. We need to understand that. It is a matter of acceptance.

The conscious mind will decide to reject or to accept this situation. When our conscious mind rejects the condition of lacking material things, we start building hate for ourselves for the situation in which we live.

We forget that we are His children and He will take care of His creatures. When we have the good fortune of owning material possessions, this is the opportunity that our Creator gives to us to share with others that which we possess. If our conscious mind rejects this idea and makes us blind to the necessity of being in contact with God, this is when we start getting in trouble with ourselves.

We cannot keep ourselves walking blind to this situation. We cannot live just complaining or keeping possessions for ourselves. The consequences of this behavior will take us to the limits of sadness, worry, and nervous collapse. Our senses will reign over our bodies and lead us to our own destruction.

Why can't we do something about this? In both situations, we have to turn ourselves to God. He is our Savior. He will indicate to us what we have to do in both cases. He will teach us compassion for ourselves and compassion for others. He will show us that the more we share, the more we receive. *Seeing is believing.*

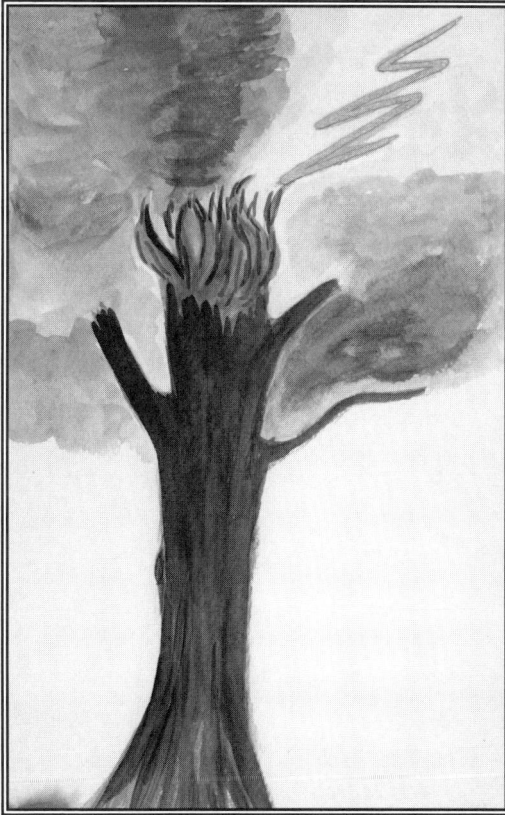

The Elements
Earth, Fire, Water, Air

Chapter 24

On Accepting Ourselves

*I*t is a disgrace to ignore the content of our soul. For what we are we should accept.

The disadvantage of being in the position of a person of color, of living in a place where this kind of human being is not accepted, plays a game in our subconscious mind.

We think that because our differences in color, we are different in our souls, too. This is a great mistake. The color of our skin has nothing to do with our soul. Souls have no color. Souls are accepted by God's Eternal Love without distinction, because we are His children and for Him we are all the same.

It is a shame when people don't realize this fact, when they put each other down because of color. We all have to understand how important it is to feel love and compassion for one another, how important it is to share this compassion with other races, how important it is to live together in this beautiful world that has been created for us to enjoy in the most peaceful possible way.

God did not create this world for the poor or the rich or for one race or another, He created it for everybody. Each of us has the right to be here, to be happy and to enjoy it with love and respect. Humankind needs to understand this.

When we allow our hate for others who are different to take over, then we are denying God's wishes. Tolerance and respect are very important qualities to apply in our daily lives. We need to understand this.

Allowing these qualities to come to us, we will find the sensation that we perceive in our hearts will be greater that any splendid material thing we can get in this world.

We will realize the consequence of healing arising from our hearts.

We will feel free of hate, and acceptance will fill our hearts.

We will sense the feeling of love in ourselves for others.

We will feel the sensation of freedom coming from within us.

Seeing is believing.

There was a man once who discriminated against people because they looked different from him. One day a black man came to him asking for work, and He sent the man away.

Hearing a negative answer, the black man started walking away, when suddenly he heard that somebody was calling to him. When he turned his head to see

144

who it was, the white man came rushing to him and asked him for forgiveness. The other man didn't understand this reaction. The white man replied to him: "Please, forgive me that I have judged you unfairly, because in my blind heart I have no love for others, just for myself."

God's Eternal Love makes no distinction among us. He is there. He loves us and accepts us as we are.

There are occasions when we become aggravated because another person does not respond to our demands, but the understanding of human differences will lead us to apply tolerance.

We have to realize that love and understanding in these situations will be much better than hate. *For what we are we shall receive.*

Chapter 25

On Achieving Our Goals

*W*e need to understand that continuing things as they are in a world full of hate and human misery will lead only to chaos and death. Consequently, we need to achieve our goal to be better. We have to continue our desire to be touched by God's Eternal Love. We have to seek Him anywhere we are. *Seeing is believing.*

When we stop our growth because we don't receive what we are asking for, then we go into depression and disillusionment, because our senses were expecting those changes, not our heart.

Being controlled by our senses is a risky game that our conscious mind plays with us. We need to be aware of our senses and the way they control us. Our senses are the manifestation of our desires, lower or higher.

When we let our lower desires control us, then we permit the abuse of our body by our conscious mind. When we live by our higher desires, our subconscious mind will tell us what to receive and accept from our body and how to guide it.

The first way will bring us unhappiness and nonacceptance of ourselves. The second way will bring us love and understanding of ourselves. Both responses will be applied to us in accordance with what we do to others. *For what we are we shall receive.* This is the law of **karma.**

Demonstrating to others how good or bad we are has no purpose, for we must first apply this law to ourselves. We have first to see in ourselves the changes we are going to make, in order to follow the path that we are seeking.

The compassion and respect that we feel for ourselves when seeking this path will be proof of the effort, understanding, and love coming from us back to us. It is a matter of self-realization. It is a matter of being convinced that the satisfaction of our senses does not lie in always pleasing them. It lies simply in the understanding, knowledge, and mastery of them.

This will bring a beautiful feeling of peace and release. It is a matter of seeing ourselves as wonderful creatures of God. It is a matter of knowing that we can do beautiful things for ourselves if we stop doubting our Creator and let Him take care of us in the way He wants. It is loving Him and just being thankful for being here in this world that He has created for our enjoyment. *Seeing is believing.*

Our body will respond to these signs of happiness with good health and joy. Anything

150

we do, little or big, will be done with pleasure and comfort. Anything we receive, little or big, will be accepted with love.

When all these changes happen we can no longer deny that we are part of our Creator and He is part of His children. We can clearly see that many of the problems we live with in this life are created by our conscious mind. We should realize this.

One has to acknowledge the fact that these problems without a proper solution will take us nowhere. That is why it is so important to make the decision to be ready for the changes to come, to be sure that these changes are what we really want for our life.

We cannot continue denying to ourselves the right to be happy. We cannot continue harming our body. We cannot continue denying the importance of keeping our soul clear of sins and close to God's Eternal Love.

Seeking perfect harmony for our soul-body-God is the direction we need to seek. In rejecting this harmony, we will continue the cycle of our problems and hates. It is a simple realization that our body will decay if our soul is not receiving the precious gift of energy from our Creator.

If we continue on the negative path, we will see that the results are not what we expect. Pushing away our belief in ourselves

151

and in God our Creator is putting our goals in danger of being lost in the darkness. Being lost in the darkness is like walking blind without a cane. Do we wish to keep ourselves in the darkness? This will be our choice.

God's Eternal Love will be waiting for us until we decide to search for His light. He will be there, waiting, and will receive us with His Divine Love and understanding and forgiveness of our faults. We have to believe this.

Chapter 26

On Believing in Ourselves

*B*elieving in ourselves, in what we are capable of doing, is very important. God teaches us the proper use of our powers. In using our powers, we realize the consequences of being different than we were before. Being different means being under the guidance of God and in control of ourselves.

Why is it that we don't want to use these powers?, why are we afraid of them? Simply because we don't know how to control them. When we use these powers, we need to be in constant contact with God. We cannot allow these powers to lead us or take us over for their purposes. We need to know what they are for.

Our perception of the good and the bad needs to be clear at all times. It is a key to seeing things clearly and to stopping negative influences from taking over.

Why is it that we do not recognize when we are using our power over others just to please our desire to show others how important we are?, why can't we stop this mistake? Because our fears lead us to use those powers to protect ourselves from being hurt, and then use these powers in a negative way.

In using our powers in a negative way,

we give away our desire to give and receive. The person who misuses his powers only gets from others, he does not receive. This power can get out of control, and will make him an abuser of power.

Using this power to give and receive will take us to the path of self-realization. It will show us that what we are doing is right, seeing the loving response that others will show towards us. *Seeing is believing.*

When we learn how to use these powers, then we can feel pride in ourselves. Then we cannot deny that we are part of God, that we do not need to suffer from guilt or love starvation any more. *Seeing is believing.*

Chapter 27

On The Healing Process

*T*he healing process of our body is in our mind. We cannot doubt this.

Why is it that we insist on harming our body?. This comes when our mind is not ready to heal our body. It will take a long period of time to heal our body if our mind is not ready to do so.

We take our body to the doctor's bed, to see what he can do about it. But we pay little attention to our soul. We forget to talk about our soul because we cannot see it and because it is nothing we can show to others with pride.

> *There was once a man who was very sick and he decided to go to the best doctor in his home town. He was explaining his incurable illness, when the doctor said to him: "I see nothing wrong in your body, but I advise you to ask yourself about the causes of this illness. Your soul will then discover the problem." Seeing is believing.*

Our body's illness will teach us what is wrong in our souls. We can control much illness by knowing ourselves and the reason for which we are suffering. Our body is our best advisor, to let us know of our errors, of our happiness or unhappiness, of good or bad actions towards ourselves or others. We cannot deny this.

Often, we let our body decay because it is too much trouble to take care of our soul. Or we prefer to fill our body with chemicals, instead of filling our soul with love and understanding for ourselves and others.

We are careless about our soul because we don't have to spend money on it. We have just to spend the time to take care of it. Our body is the most precious gift of our Creator, and we throw it away, like a piece of garbage that we don't need.

We spend time and money on doctors, but we don't spend time on our soul. We doubt the returns of spending time on our soul. The reason for acting in this way comes from not accepting ourselves. We don't love ourselves, because of our feeling of guilt, and the only way we see of destroying that feeling is to destroy the visible object, our body.

Peace

Chapter 28

On Our Desire for Material Possessions

*F*rom generation to generation, we continue the desire for material possessions, without thinking about the consequences. There is nothing wrong in having possessions, when we know that they are not going to possess us.

We have to be in God's Grace to possess material things and keep ourselves in the purity and simple life that will be demanded of us. We cannot deny this.

We cannot live in opulence when we are honestly in contact with God. When we seek His Eternal Love, we have to be clear inside of desires and to be ready for the changes to come.

Some will ask themselves: "Why do I need to be clear and without desires when seeking God's Eternal Love? Does He not accept everybody just the way they are?"

That is the truth, but we need to make some offering to Him as well, and that offering is to open our heart with sincerity and our own strong desire to be different.

Why can't we continue living in opulence and be with God as well? Because one does not match with the other.

Just look at nature's perfection, the color of the flowers matches perfectly with the color of the grass. Just look at the sky, the color of the clouds matches perfectly with the color of the sky. That is God's perfection. Why can't man be attuned to nature, when he knows that he is part of His creation?

Man always finds excuses to keep himself in the darkness. He forgets that God's Eternal Love wants this perfection in him, too. Man needs to be prepared to offer his purity of heart and his sincerity of desire when seeking Him. *Seeing is believing.*

Why are we so afraid of renouncing material things?

Why can't we give more importance to our love of God?

Why should we be ashamed of ourselves, when others cannot see that we are for Him and not only for ourselves?

Because we are lost in the world of material things, where what is important is not the soul, but only our bodies. We cannot deny this.

Chapter 29

On Honesty Towards Ourselves as the Best Rule

When we realize that our behavior is taking us along a negative path, then it is time to look at ourselves and see that we are neglecting our soul. We need to demand an explanation to ourselves and to find out what the problem is. It is a matter of time, and of responsibility.

When our reaction goes against the desire to see within ourselves, then we need to recognize that we are not ready to face reality, because our fears are still in control of our soul. When we recognize that we need to accept our problems, and we seek a solution from within, then we are facing reality and we are entitled to receive the help that we are seeking. Honesty towards ourselves is the best rule.

Why are we so afraid of finding our own faults? Because it is so difficult to face them and to accept them. We forget that if we do so, every thing will be all right, that a heavy weight will be lifted from our back if we just recognize them, accept them, and deal with them in the way God's Eternal Love demands. *Seeing is believing.*

There was a man once who committed one fault after another.

Every time he went to his temple to pray, he said to his God: "You see here one of the worst sinners in the whole world, but I am not proud of what I am doing. I ask of your Divine Mercy to help me take this heavy weight off of my back."
In response to his honesty, God told him: "Go in peace, your sins are forgiven."

If we have the courage to recognize our errors, and the honest desire to have them taken away, then we gain a lot of time for ourselves. Letting the errors stay in us and take over is a mistake that we pay for heavily. *Seeing is believing.*

Chapter 30

On Relationships

*I*n relationships, respect is very important. We need to understand this. When we give our love to another person, we share part of our deepest beliefs as well. The need to love and be loved reflects our own desire for companionship. We cannot deny this.

We have to understand that this need has to be reciprocated, otherwise it will be lost in selfishness and misinterpretations. In consequence, to have a harmonious relationship we need to be in harmony inside ourselves.

When we are not ready to fulfill this purpose, the relationship will become like a nightmare, in which we are unprepared to solve the oncoming problems. It is necessary for us to be ready spiritually and have the courage to face these problems.

Tolerance is very important to keep a relationship going, for it is one of the finest proofs of each other's love. Reasoning together about each other's mistakes is the best way to arrive at a good understanding.

Why it is so difficult for some couples to reach at this point? Because the intolerance coming from both sides, the lack of forgiveness, the desire to keep themselves always together, makes it difficult.

173

When the spiritual life is fulfilled, it is a matter of common friendship and problems will be solved more easily. *Seeing is believing.*

Communication of any kind of difficulty or problem arising in our relationships must occur without avoidance or delay. When we have no desire to continue a relationship it is because there is no love from either side. For a harmonious relationship there must be love, and love requires tolerance.

Chapter 31

On Rules

*W*e cannot function just to please others. Our life needs to be focussed on something we believe in that is stronger than ourselves. We are very vulnerable souls.

We cannot keep changing our minds constantly, because the distortion of our power will take us over.

It is very important for us to set rules and follow them. Children are a good example of this. We set rules for children in order for them to listen to our words and discipline. They will follow our rules in the best way they can.

Parents feel satisfaction in seeing obedience come from their children. Children see that life will be easier when the family follows rules of respect and obedience.

This example applies to human behavior, no matter what the age. God's Eternal Love has given us this world to enjoy, but He has set rules for us to respect and to love. We, as His children, need to follow these rules very carefully. He will help us as a good parent will. He will show us the best way to Him. We need to understand this.

When children deny to themselves that following the rules that have been set for them by their parents is for their own good, then they experience how everything can be turned upside down for them.

When people don't follow God's rules, they will see truly how their lives will become confused. *Seeing is believing.*

Nature is a great example of fidelity to her own rules. Man, in his own desire for power, likes to overcome or disregard these rules. In his superior position as a human being, he thinks that he can do everything he wants to demonstrate his power over his fellow man and over nature.

What a big mistake!. We don't need to demonstrate any position of superiority over anyone or anything to be accepted and loved by others.

Things in nature work in harmony with God's Divine Love. Things in nature will not destroy themselves or others just for the pleasure of doing so. Man needs to understand and learn from this.

Things in nature are the most beautiful example of love and coordination. It is very important for us to live and be in daily contact with nature, our best teacher. We live our lives under the constant pressure of daily problems, and we forget Nature. What a good friend Nature is!

In our selfish life we forget that we are a great part of Nature. We are not playing our own role well. We think time is more important for doing something else, rather than contemplating Nature. When we don't understand, we become careless. If we take care of Nature, she will return our care with respect, beauty, and health. If we don't work together with Nature, we will know the result in catastrophes, hunger, and illness. It is God's law.

Freedom

Chapter 32

On Controlling Our Actions to Find Directions

*M*any times we ask ourselves: Why do I behave this way?

Everything has a reason. We think: Why do circumstances make us react in ways that we dislike? Because we are running our lives in the opposite direction from what is supposed to be. Because we haven't given direction to ourselves. We need to control our actions. This is a clear statement of how mistaken we are in our behavior, and how far we are from putting order into our actions. We need to understand this.

It is really amazing how we can live without any direction. Who can control our actions if we don't have direction or belief? It is necessary to find ourselves through our Creator. It is important for us to have faith and to believe that our Creator is waiting for us, to ask Him to guide our steps. It is very important for us to have the feeling of love and understanding in our hearts.

If we reject this beautiful feeling, our life will have no meaning, our steps will be lost in the darkness, and our heart will be closed to God's Eternal Love. *Seeing is believing.*

It is very important to have this faith in order to communicate with our Creator and with our fellow brothers and sisters.

It is very important to have this faith in order to keep our families together in love and tolerance.

It is very important to have this faith in order to feel compassion in our hearts for ourselves and others.

It is very important to have this faith in order to give and receive with others in a mutual exchange of energy and love. We cannot deny this.

Truth emanates from our Creator.

Chapter 33

On The Senses as a Very Important Part of Our Body Systems

*T*he senses are a very important part of our body system. The senses will lead us properly if we know how to control them, or they will lead us far astray if we do not know how to control them. We need to understand that the senses are connected to our feelings in an important way. It is a matter of knowing how our senses work. If we let them take over, we will find ourselves acting as their slave. If we let them come under our control, they will open many beautiful feelings up to us.

We must try to understand the reason why there are people in this world who cannot find happiness, even though they have everything, or have nothing. They are slaves to the senses. The best time to recognize how our senses are controlling us is when we try to please all the desires our body asks for.

After a desire has been satisfied then boredom and unhappiness takes over. This is when we realize that we have been doing something that did not please our heart as well.

When we respond to our senses in a more positive way, our feeling is totally different. We feel happy and fulfilled, we feel recharged and satisfied with ourselves, we see that life is beautiful and we give thanks to our Creator for this. *Seeing is believing.*

There are circumstances in life in which we don't know how to respond to our senses, whether to please or not to please them. This situation requires being honest with ourselves and learning to appreciate things in a genuine way. The senses can be pleased in doing something to help others.

When we see need coming from another person and our heart is moved to help, there will be a kind of internal satisfaction of our senses when the action is done with love and compassion. *Seeing is believing.*

> *There was a man once who was very unhappy and bored of seeing himself just being at home doing his regular duties.*
> *One day he heard from a friend that a poor family of ten children was having financial trouble in meeting their needs to survive.*
> *The man thought: "Well, it is not my business that this family is in trouble!" Then, in a moment of compassion, he decided to go and help them, both with friendship and material help. When he returned home, his feelings of*

boredom and unhappiness had disappeared.

He found out through his action that we cannot live an empty existence, that we need to fulfill our senses through positive actions for ourselves and for others. *For what we are we shall receive.*

The World

Chapter 34

On Working in Harmony with Our Creator

*I*f we work in total harmony with our Creator, our problems will be solved more easily. We cannot deny this.

We realize the human necessity of being in constant contact with Him. When we suffer extreme desperation, then we think about Him. Otherwise, we totally ignore Him. Our Creator does not want this from us, to be ignored, He is there, always, waiting. *Seeing is believing.*

When we decide to get in touch with Him, we will be not disappointed. We will see how exact His answers to our questions are, we will see how well He will help us with our problems, little and big. We will see how He helps us without expecting material things in return, just our love for Him.

If people will just believe in His Love for one second of time, they will feel how powerful it is. They will feel comforted and peaceful. They will feel energetic and harmonious with themselves and toward others. It will create a feeling of peace and harmony among us, and the world will be the most beautiful Paradise to live in.

If we just let Him touch us, we will be the blessed ones in the Universe. In consequence, in denying His presence we condemn ourselves to live with wars, mental disorders, hate, spiritual poverty, and unhappiness. We cannot deny this.

Look at nature. It is not separate from the Creator. This is why nature is so harmonious. Man needs to understand this, and try to follow Nature's steps in order to find God's Grace. When we detach ourselves from Nature and God's Grace we are the ones who lose, because we cannot continue living without them, alone.

We are part of the whole system, God-Nature. We cannot, in our arrogance, pretend that we can live just with our own power and selfishness. We are His creation and Nature is His creation. He will be the one who decides what is good or bad for us, not ourselves. Man's arrogance cannot conquer the world. It is God's Law.

Chapter 35

On Denying God's Existence

*W*hen we deny God's existence, we are denying our own existence.

When we doubt God's Eternal Love, we are doubting our ability to love.

When we doubt God's Compassion, we are doubting our own compassion for ourselves and others.

Why do we choose to live so miserably and unhappily?

Because we don't understand that we are part of God's Creation.

Because we don't want to face the responsibility of being part of His Creation.

Because we don't want to recognize Him as our Creator. *Seeing is believing.*

When we doubt Him, we are pleasing our ego by thinking we are superior to everything He has created.

When we reject His presence in us, we are rejecting the desire to be like Him.

In consequence, we reject our desire to be better for the desire to be powerful by controlling others and gaining material possessions. We cannot deny this. *For what we are we shall receive.*

When conditions make things possible for us, then we are pleased. We quickly forget who we are and why we are here, and who gives us the right to be here.

The conscious mind is very skillful in helping us forget all these things! The conscious mind, our best ally, will also be our bad counselor in solving problems or facing difficult situations alone. Our conscious mind will please our senses first, before we face God's presence. *Seeing is believing.*

In our desire to posses material things, we often lose sight of the existence of our Creator, and when we reach the point when material possessions do no fill us up, then we start seeking our Divine Creator once more.

We established a rivalry between beliefs. "Do I belief in what I see, or what I don't see?". What I see and touch gives securities to my senses, what I don't see and I cannot touch creates in me uncertainty and doubt.

Why do I have to put up with something that makes me feel insecure?

It is very hard to try to convince a person who just acts and thinks with the senses, not with the heart. *For what we are we shall received.*

Sometimes, when something terrible is about to happen, the soul can react in such a strong way that belief without touching or seeing occurs. That soul will be changed for ever, and will fight against anyone who has the same doubt that he had before. We can call this a "miracle". Some will call it an "act of magic". These miracles are just small signs of the love from our Creator to us.

Some will call it an "act of chance", when it is simple the way God shows His Eternal Love to us. Some will call it "a simple coincidence", but this is the way that He shows His existence to us. In exchange for these miracles, He simply desires the love and respect from His children. Is that too much to ask?.

Jesus, the Divine Man of Love, was an example of the perfection incarnated in the pure love and respect for His Lord and His creation.

Why it is so difficult for us to follow His words? Because our lack of belief and understanding of such things called "miracles".

Chapter 36

On Those Who Wish to See the Light of God

*F*or those who wish to see the Light of God's Eternal Love, He will be with them. Those who deny God's existence, will find themselves in the darkness of their own decisions.

When we make the decision of living apart from our Creator, it is a choice that we make and we have to live with. We are here in this world to make choices. We are our own decision-makers. God is there, waiting. We cannot deny this. In consequence, any decision we make is our responsibility.

Many times we don't wish to be responsible for our own decisions. Then we blame our mistakes on God or on somebody else. This is an easy way to run our lives. But at the end of the run we are the only ones who suffer, by losing the right to be happy. It is our own choice.

Centering ourselves in the Magnificence of God's Eternal Love, we are chosen for the most beautiful gift we will ever receive in life. It is a Gift that cannot be compared with any other valuable thing in the whole world. *Seeing is believing.*

The communication we establish with our Creator has no comparison. We cannot deny this.

In moments of depression, unhappiness or discontent, we think of calling or visiting a friend or relative to communicate our problems, but we don't think of having a private dialogue with our Creator. He will listen to us, with no excuse of being too time consuming. *For what we are we shall receive.*

There are occasions when we don't know what to do about our problems and we just want to keep them to ourselves without telling anyone what they are about.

From our Creator we can have no secrets, for He knows everything and He is looking upon us, just waiting to be called. We should not close our minds and hearts to Him, for He is our Creator and our Savior.

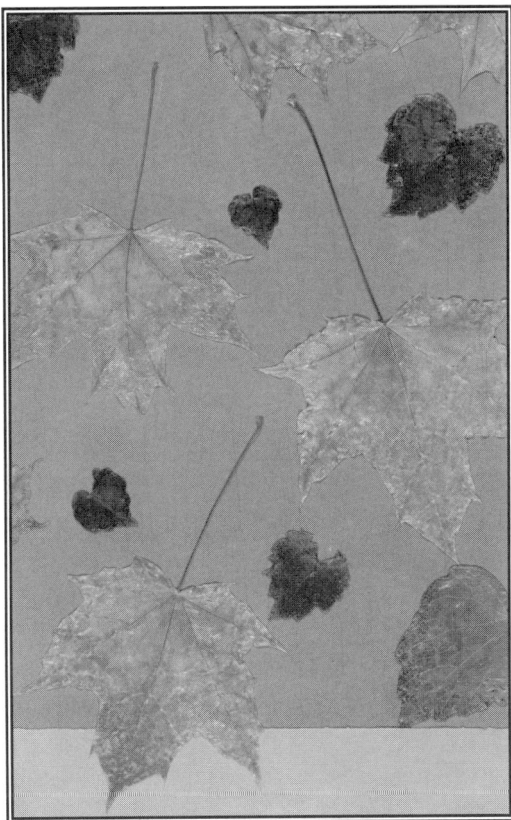

Fall

Chapter 37

On Living a Materialistic Life-Style

*I*f we direct our lives only in a materialistic way, we are directing our souls to unhappiness. We cannot live by thinking, acting, and desiring to become the most perfect and powerful creatures in the world.

The price to be paid for this arrogance of mind will be very high. We need to come down from our desires and control our senses. Then the arrogance will be released little by little from our souls.

When we make a decision to be different, we are making a decision to be ready for the changes to come in our lives. If we put things aside to be done tomorrow, we delay the time to move closer to our Creator, to be guided and loved by Him.

In our blind arrogance we don't see this reality because we are not interested in things that we cannot see or touch. *Seeing is believing.*

To deny this truth to ourselves, is to deny the right of being with Him. It is a matter of true religious belief to accept Him, and we all need this truth. We cannot deny this.

If we just permit ourselves a second of time in our lives to imagine letting go of material things and having the touch of God's

Eternal Love, we will realize what we are missing. *Seeing is believing.*

> *There was a man once whose only desire was to become rich and to have his life free from trouble in the future. When he was very near his goal, he noticed that the thing he was living for had no meaning. Then he decided that the money he had accumulated all those years, he would give away to help others in need. After this, he could not believe the change and happiness he felt in his heart. From that moment, his life found the meaning of brotherhood. He found the meaning of being important in helping others. He found the meaning of being different. He found the meaning of self-realization, of compassion, and of love for himself and others. For what we are we shall receive.*

If we decide that our life has no sense to be lived, it is a reflection of our lack of appreciation for ourselves. Sometimes our life doesn't make any sense to us, we can't find any meaning to it. If we give ourselves a little time to look more closely, then we will see why. Our life makes no sense to us because of the emptiness, the indolence and passivity. We cannot deny this.

We involve ourselves in the emptiness of an easy lifestyle. We have no control over our senses, and we are careless about what surround us, the Light of our Creator. We think that by getting fashionable things, or making new advances in our careers of professions, we will be fully satisfied and will forget our obligations to ourselves and to our Lord. *Seeing is believing.*

Oh Divine love, help us to find your Light that will guide us in this darkness!

Chapter 38

On Assuming not Deserving God's Eternal Love

*T*he conditions that lead us to assume that we are not deserving of God's Eternal Love come from our own desire to feel sorry for ourselves. We hold to this self-pity in order to follow the path of pain and suffering that has been created since our birth. We will always look for a reason to feel it, and to let others see it. What we see and feel as sadness or bad luck, is our own desires reflected in our self-pity.

Our desire for personal growth is very important, for it will help us continue along a positive path of happiness and self-assurance. We need to have this positive attitude in order to know how to survive in the days to come. *Seeing is believing.*

If we don't choose this positive path for ourselves as a matter of survival, we may see our efforts crumble. Sometimes we say: This life is for the stronger one to live. When we say that, we are giving away everything, including the desire to be different.

Why it is so easy for us to abandon the desire to be better just because of an obstacle that we find in our way? Because our desires and thoughts are so weak that we lack the strength to put this obstacle to the side and keep going. *For what we are we shall receive.*

Can we do something about this? Yes. When we make a decision to work through a problem, to change habits, to be different, this decision needs to be made with a strong desire to follow the guidelines that we are setting up for ourselves.

We cannot just put them aside when we want to, or when we get tired, or because we feel it is impossible to follow them. This is the moment when our strength has to come out, to show us that we can do it.

When we see the results of the strength coming from our change of behavior, we should give thanks to ourselves for what we have done. When we follow principles of strength and discipline, we are not following them for anybody else, but for ourselves.

When we receive the rewards coming from this strength, the joy of seeing what we have done will be part of our own appreciation, no one else's.

Chapter 39

On Ignoring Our Creator

*T*he conditions that make a man do things or behave in a way that he doesn't want are related to the situation in which he is living at a particular moment. When we don't know how to control these situations, we reach the point of exhausting our energy. When we exhaust our energy source and we don't know how to replenish it, then we will suffer from energy starvation. It is like a plant that you ignore and forget to give water and light. It will starve in a matter of days. Man will suffer the same process unless he takes care of himself.

Food is important, but nothing is more important and necessary than energy. Food will give us the energy we need for our body to function, but the energy we need for our soul to function comes from our Creator. *Seeing is believing.*

When we ignore our Creator, we will begin to suffer from energy starvation. The results will show when our body begins to decay. The body will respond to energy starvation with illness, dissatisfaction, and feeling uncomfortable, no matter where we move it or place it. These are the first symptoms of energy starvation. When we ignore these symptoms and we keep going on and on, the weakness will spread.

When we become aware of this energy starvation, we may realize that if we take care of this, we can be spared from painful illness or bodily problems.

Why do we wait until the last minute to take care of ourselves? Because of our own ignorance in regard to our soul and body system. Because we are careless about our spiritual growth. Because we think that the pleasure of our senses alone will keep us healthy and happy.

The Rape of the Sea

Chapter 40

On Living Our Lives in Disharmony with Ourselves

We often continue living our lives in complete disharmony with ourselves.

Why don't we do something about this? Because we are used to hurting ourselves, because we aren't used to living without feeling that we deserve to suffer pain, because we feel hate toward ourselves and think that the best way of paying for having low karma it is through suffering. *Seeing is believing.*

If a film were to pass in front of our eyes showing all our actions, we would be amazed at how much time we spend in suffering.

There are so many other good things to do for ourselves and others to occupy our minds and our time!

Why don't we occupy our time and our minds in doing these things? Because we feel unbalanced. When we feel totally happy, we think about a negative situation right at that moment, because this sense of happiness feels wrong.

We cannot be happy today because we feel something not so good is going to happen to us tomorrow.

This is what humankind thinks about happiness. Isn't it amazing?

The peaceful happiness that comes from

our spiritual growth cannot be compared with anything from the material world. It is a well-balanced happiness. It is a healthy body responding to that happiness. It is in the way our eyes look at things. It is in the way we enjoy our senses, without being afraid of losing control or being possessed by them.

A simple glass of water that we drink in that moment of spiritual happiness will be most delightful. The most simple thing will be the most wonderful thing to enjoy. *Seeing is believing.*

Chapter 41

On Illness

*I*n making our body only an instrument of pleasure, we are casting away the purity that God's Eternal Love has given to us as our birthright. The consequences, the problems, and disappointments that come to us from this behavior, will be our own responsibility. *Seeing is believing.*

> *There was a man once who could not stop his sexual appetite. He was in such hurry to satisfy his desire, that one day he contracted an incurable and contagious disease. Seeing himself in this terrible situation, he tried to blame his problem on his own body for having this extreme sexual appetite. Then his awareness spoke to him: "Why do you blame your weakness on the instrument that you are using only for pleasure? Just think a little and see who is controlling whom." For what we are we shall receive.*

In demanding excess pleasure for our body, we are denying the right to be healthy.

Body and mind need to work together. It is God's Law. When we deny this truth to ourselves, we are pushing ourselves towards decadency as a human society. In corrupting our bodies and souls, our morals decay. *Seeing is believing.*

Why don't we do something about this? Because of our lack of self-esteem, we lack the courage to stop this behavior. Because we think that the pleasures of the body have more importance than anything that is spiritual. We cannot deny this.

Sometimes we expect things to work well without any effort on our part. Where does this lethargic attitude come from? It comes from our desire not to spend any time from our daily life on spiritual matters. *Seeing is believing.*

We leave this kind of thing to be done tomorrow, and that tomorrow will never come. Spiritual matters. They are quite a joke for us.

Who cares about being good to ourselves and others?

Who cares to be in God's Grace or to be loved by Him?

Who is He, anyway?

It is this lethargy and passive attitude which puts us apart from the spiritual path.

What a waste of time!

When we look at ourselves in the

mirror, don't we worry about who we are? Then we say: Who cares!

Oh God! forgive us for what we do to ourselves.........

In fact, the characteristics of being in a poor spiritual condition are very clear to the perceptive person. The color of the skin has no glow or radiance, and the eyes have a sad look to them. A simple person can detect that these consequences are caused by an illness. A doctor may detect it in the body. In consequence, if we look at ourselves in the mirror, it will be easy for us to detect this illness within our soul.

When we change our attitude and become responsible for ourselves, the tone of our skin and the expression of our eyes will change, too. *Seeing is believing.*

In the same way that our body becomes sick, so does our soul. Healing the physical part will be not as helpful as healing the spiritual part from the start.

God's Eternal Love is the only power that can heal our soul. We cannot deny that.

But we say: I don't understand where I can find Him. I go to church regularly. I confess my sins. I take communion. I am a good person. But it seems to me that He does not care about my bad situation. Very well, but do we perform these actions honestly, or just to act for others, to follow rules and customs of society?

Without looking too far, you can find God's Eternal Love in the God that is within you. We can contact Him anytime we wish. We can have an inner dialogue with Him any day, anytime when we need it.

He can radiate His love through us so that people can see it. He is the pure and the strong energy that we all need to keep functioning in this world. He is our lover, our family, our best friend, who will never abandon us, no matter what the circumstances we are living in the moment. He is our time, our space, our world. No question will be without an answer when we are living His path of Light.

Why is it so difficult for us to establish this contact with Him?

There is a simple answer: Because our beliefs about Him are false, and full of doubts. Because of our lack of faith in ourselves. And because we call Him just when we are in need, and do not seek him as part of our everyday companionship.

When we stimulate our glandular system, we will discover that the whole system works in union with our pineal gland. When our endocrine system is abused for whatever reason, bodily disorganization and decay will follow. Our endocrine system is very delicate and its functions are very

236

important to us. When our endocrine system works perfectly, our behavior will be the result of that perfection. It is our job to keep these glands working in harmony unless their malfunction was caused at the time we were born or by genetic complications.

How can we keep our endocrine system working in harmony? By controlling our actions. For example, our temper. If we can keep our temper controlled with diet and exercise, our adrenal glands will respond to this. When we keep our sexual life under control, active but without abuse, we will keep ourselves away from pernicious illness. We cannot deny this.

We cannot deny that spiritual contact with God will save us from decadency of the body. When we choose not to have contact with our Creator, we are pushing ourselves to our imminent end, corruption and decay of our soul and body. *For what we are we shall receive.*

God will teach us how to keep ourselves together and strong until we reach the peace and happiness that He has ready for us. Yet, we keep denying His presence and love to ourselves. This is the reason we make it so hard for ourselves.

Oh, infinite Love! Help us to find your Divine Light before we do great harm to ourselves.

Chapter 42

On Self-Esteem

When we see ourselves begging for love from another human being in a relationship, it is because our self-compassion and self-esteem is running very low. It is a shame that we have to stop so low looking for love.

The Love coming from our Creator is so pure that we don't have to beg for it. It is just there, waiting for us. His love is unconditional. His love will begin in our heart. His love will rejuvenate us with His Light. His love will be our daily bread that supports our soul and our body. His love will enhance our body and make it healthy, more healthy each day.

When we choose to suffer because of the lack of love from another human being, we do all the most impossible things to attract his or her attention. If these things do not work, our disappointment and suffering take us over. We close ourselves to any contact with the outside world.

Running away from reality will not help us rectify our errors. When we have the courage to put all the pieces together, then we can realize that we have no need to keep suffering. *Seeing is believing.*

When we choose to continue living in

the nightmare we have created, the suffering will become deeper and deeper until we will reach the point that our body responds with illness.

Can we do something about this negative behavior?

Yes. We can open our eyes and our heart and see the reality inside. We can help ourselves by simply turning our eyes and heart to our Creator. He will show us the way to proceed. He will stay with us, with His love and companionship expecting little in return. We will feel His presence among us when we need it most. We will never feel lonely or abandoned, because His Love will be with us for ever and ever.

Chapter 43

On Family

*F*amily members. Friends. Enemies. Companions. We call them different by types of names.

Parents. They are the ones who help us come into this world. Through reincarnation, we know that we are the ones who choose them. We need to accept this responsibility.

When something doesn't work out with them, we blame them, because we don't want to accept our responsibility. *What we are we shall receive.*

Parents. They nurture us, they feed us, they help us to grow, they try to provide as much as they can, to help us in our necessities. *Seeing is believing.*

Some do this job in a better way, some in a mediocre way. But they usually try to provide the best they can. We cannot deny this.

Brothers and sisters. Some we recognize, some are totally new for us. It is like living in a community. We don't know everybody there, but we can learn to accept, love, and be tolerant and helpful to each other.

Our karma plays a very important role in the family unit. *For what we are we shall receive.*

Parents can be helpful to direct or control our behavior to adjust to the family, but we are the only ones who can do our best to become accepted and happy.

When we arrive at the age of reasoning, it will be easier for us to recognize our good and bad habits or karma.

With love and understanding from both sides, family members and ourselves, we can work through our karma.

Some children are more aware than others of their own problems. Parents can be helpful guides for us in this hard task of finding ourselves. Otherwise, it will be our job alone to search for this awareness that we seek. When we choose not to face this responsibility, then the chance that we have to redeem our karma will be wasted.

In coming here we all have that chance. If we ignore it, our own growth will suffer.

Chapter 44

On Karma

*T*o understand human behavior, we need to understand karma, and vice-versa.

Karma is an Eastern word used to describe our own behavior and our attitude toward others.

Some people work through their karma very well. Some have little knowledge of what karma means. Some know the meaning, but ignore it anyway for their own satisfaction or complacency. *Seeing is believing.*

For those who don't know what karma is and how it works in our souls, one can say that it is a way we program our actions towards others. We need to be conscious about our behavior towards others, if we don't wish to receive negative consequences later on as a result of the ignorance of our actions.

When we deny this truth, we are denying to ourselves the right to the perfection of our soul.

Jesus said: "Do unto others as you would have others do unto you." This is the law of karma. *For what we are we shall receive.*

If we are aware of our karma, then we will have the conscious choice to decide what is right or wrong to do. Our attitude toward ourselves and others will tell us when to act or when to stop our negative behavior. Awareness will register in our subconscious mind to let us know if is all right to continue on the immediate path we are following. *Seeing is believing.*

It is possible that we deny others the right to life, by intention or by accident. We need to be aware of this karma, of returning in goodness what we owe to other souls. It is the law of karma. *For what we are we shall receive.*

At the beginning of our creation, people devoted themselves to the Creator's Laws. Now that we are so far away from Him, we need to be more conscious in following His teachings and laws. We cannot deny this. *For what we are we shall receive.*

In denying this truth, we are denying to ourselves Jesus' words:

"An eye for an eye and a tooth for a tooth."

When we deny this truth, we are allowing ourselves to do things that we should avoid. Respect and tolerance should be practiced at all times. For this positive behavior will help us to control our senses and our reactions. As a human being with the right to choose what is good or bad, we are more aware of our actions than other animals.

When we don't follow these rules of

behavior, then we choose to condemn ourselves to chaos. *Seeing is believing.*

When we don't accept the consequences of our actions, we are denying to ourselves the opportunity to redeem our karma. Facing these consequences and responsibilities will help us to grow and find the right path for us. *Seeing is believing.*

When we doubt karma, we are allowing ourselves to continue on the wrong path. *For what we are we shall receive.*

When we search for God's Eternal Love, we need to be clear and to have the strong desire to clear our karma. It is a matter of belief and understanding.

This is why it is so important that we be careful in what we do to others and to ourselves right now. This is why it is so important to be in God's Grace. He will help us to stop our negative desires to destroy or hurt others. He will show us the Light of being in His Grace. He will prevent us from doing things that will bring us negative karma.

This necessity of being in His Grace is a very important matter to humanity. It is a matter of the preservation of the soul.

A good example of ignoring God's Grace could be made with a piece of food that we want to eat later. We need to preserve it, wrapping it well and putting it in the right place, so that it will not get spoiled or contaminated. Who wants to eat something that has become poison to our body because we didn't take care of it? Nobody will eat it.

Is the same with our soul. If we don't take care of it, and it is filled with hates and problems, our body will be the one that suffers the consequences of this poison. *Seeing is believing.*

God's Eternal Love will be the preserver of our soul. He will not let it spoil or become a rotten poison to us or to others.

Nature knows very well how He takes care of her.

If people were able to spend a few minutes of their precious time to contemplate and observe the miracle of preservation in Nature, emanating from God's Eternal Love, they would understand this easily.

Tears of pain come to God's eyes when He sees the destruction of Nature coming from the hands of man, and the destruction of man coming from his own actions.

Without Name

*Thru the eye of the rifle
man cannot see beauty*

Chapter 45

On Faith

We need to understand that nothing in this world will have more importance and value that our love for our Creator. When people realize this, the whole system of how we are living will change. *Seeing is believing.*

Every moment of our life, every minute we take to deny this truth, will be seen as wasteful. *For what we are we shall receive.*

In making a true decision to change our negative behavior, we will be taking a step towards gaining happiness and a healthy life. Negativity added to our thoughts is darkness applied to our lives. Positive energy applied to our thoughts is light that we give to our hearts and to our minds. Both are such simple rules of survival, that any person can understand them without too much effort.

Nobody needs to be of superior intellect or to have formal degrees of learning in order to understand the laws of God's Eternal Love.

We need only to be simple of heart to know the way that will take us to fulfillment.

We need only to desire to be good to ourselves and others in order to taste the sweetness of His Love.

We need only to persevere in following His Laws to know the feeling of love and being loved.

We need only to love and respect Nature in order to receive the benefits that we are entitled to as part of His creation.

We need only to be responsible for our actions and thoughts in order to ensure that our karma will be stimulated by love, not hate.

Oh, Divine Love! Help us to follow these principles faithfully, that we may have no time to get lost, or to be tempted by thoughts of negativity and hate!

When we reach towards God, we need to direct our prayers with an open mind. When we send prayers, doubting the results, we are just wasting our time. *Seeing is believing.*

God will listen when our heart and mind are truly open to Him. We need to realize that our life is based on our own behavior.

If we pray, asking for a change, and we continue with our negative actions, then we are just wasting time and effort. Everything is connected. Our actions and desires are connected.

When everything works in simultaneous way, the answer to our prayers will come and we will see the result. The substance of that result is faith.

Faith is a strong belief we need to have in order to continue living in this world. Faith in change for our own good.

Faith in our love for ourselves and others.
Faith in the results of our prayers.
Faith in what we ask God to provide us.
Faith in our body, in its functions and reactions.
Faith in our soul, in love and forgiveness.
Faith in Mother Nature as provider.
Faith in giving and receiving.
Faith in God our Creator and His infinite Love for His children.

"WHAT WE ARE WE SHALL RECEIVE"

*T*his could be symbolic words for some people, or just words without any meaning for others. These words are a testimony to our belief. If we deny believing in them, we are saying to ourselves that the teachings of God's Eternal Love are something that we need not trust or follow.

Trust! What a difficult word to understand! This word has deep meaning.

Why can't we understand it?

Because we don't trust ourselves, and this is the place where everything must begin.

How can we trust someone else's teachings when we don't trust ourselves?

Jesus was a man who trusted his people exactly in the same way He trusted himself, and He trusted his Creator.

When we persist in our lack of confidence and trust in God's Eternal Love, our confidence will decline day after day, as the snow melts with the sun. *Seeing is believing.*

How is it possible to stop this behavior of not trusting God and ourselves? With the strong desire to be changed, to love, and to be happy. This will be the key to open the door that will take us to the Paradise that is waiting for us. Don't you wish to be there?

When we see what we are doing to ourselves and to our environment, we can see that something is going wrong, but we don't want to accept it.

The pollution of our souls reflects the pollution of our bodies, which reflects the pollution of our environment. All are one in a web of destruction. *For what we are we shall receive.*

Man in his blindness and selfish behavior cannot see the point where his behavior is leading. The destruction of himself and his planet can be the end result of his worries, ambitions, and egotism.

Oh God, my Lord, why it is so difficult for humankind to contact you and to seek your love and help, before all these things come to be!

Why can't man look for your Divine Energy to connect himself to a renewed Life?

Why is man so egotistic that he doesn't want to see reality, just his own fantasies?

Why can't man open his awareness to love and understand in order to help and protect himself?

Why can't man follow the steps of Mother Nature to learn respect and develop beauty in himself?

Why can't man give one second of his time to look to the sky and see that His Divine Image is looking at him with eyes of compassion expressed through the beauty of a sunset, rain, or sunrise?

"SEEING IS BELIEVING"

What a beautiful statement.

As human beings, too often we dedicate our lives to not trusting or believing in anything that we cannot see or touch. How sad!

The Universe, our beautiful planet, ourselves, our power, our love, our God - where do all these creations come from?. From something that we do not see and cannot touch.

If we believe in our awareness and in ourselves, we will perceive the power that is within us. We will clearly perceive the Universe and our world that it is part of it.

We will see ourselves as a part of that whole. We will see and perceive ourselves as a part of God's creation. In our ignorance, we let all these perceptions pass by in exchange for what we can only touch and see.

Just recall how many times you have denied your spiritual path of growth in exchange for something material that you could enjoy seeing and touching.

Recall how many times you have stopped your spiritual contact with God within you, because you couldn't see or touch something.

This is the way in which we trade our soul, which we cannot see, for the things that we can see. This is why it is so easy to renounce our spiritual growth and replace it with material desires. *Seeing is believing.*

We are so attached to material things, that fear takes control of us if we lose them. *For what we are we shall receive.*

When we face disappointment in our lives, then we start wondering why we are here in this world, and what our mission is on earth.

It is very important to find our mission.

But some may say: How can I identify myself, how am I to know who am I?

By looking for ourselves in the search for the God that is within.

When we lose this identification, then we lose ourselves.

When we detach ourselves from this God, we lose the connection with our Creator.

Our Creator, God's Eternal Love, will keep this flame burning when we are in contact with the God that is within us.

When this flame goes out for any reason, then we find ourselves in darkness.

We must remember that we always have the choice to rekindle the flame once again, no matter what the situation, no matter what the circumstance. God's Eternal Love is always there, waiting for our decision to go back to Him. *Seeing is believing.*

Oh, Divine Light! Keep us in the light until our mission is fulfilled. Help us to keep away from hurting others, from hatred and selfish behavior, that our hearts may always shine with Your Love that is our love and Your Tolerance that is our tolerance for ourselves and others.

Conclusion

Sometimes we find ourselves wondering if our knowledge of God's Eternal Love is complete, or if it really exists in our hearts. We doubt whether to believe or not to believe it. It is essential for all human beings to have knowledge about who we really are and where we really come from.

It will be like a child who has been born and has been abandoned by his parents. He will wander about, trying to find his own identity, and a parent with whom he can identify himself.

In the same way, man needs to identify himself with some kind of belief that suits him. This is the reason why man has created religion, and myths - to have roots where he can go back to when he loses himself.

When a man rejects the past beliefs he has known, he needs to go back and discover the roots of faith that will nurture him and help him make a new beginning.

A man who has been condemned by society for any particular reason, can start

269

looking at the roots of his belief and he will find out that he is not alone, that there is something in him that will give him the light and the reason to start a new life. *Seeing is believing.*

In finding God's Light, we arrive at the point of finding ourselves.

Every moment of our lives that we spend in this effort will be a moment of our life that will be rewarded. *For what we are we shall receive.*

When we use our senses to search for His Divine Love, instead of ignoring it or rejecting it, our senses will open to the most beautiful feelings of love and self-assurance. We will learn that all the sensations we felt before are nothing compared with this new feeling.

Can we allow ourselves one day to feel this way without fear of losing something?

Be assured that when we get in touch with our Creator we lose our fear, and in losing our fear we gain self-assurance.

When we are sure about ourselves and who we are and where we come from, and we know how important it is for us to establish this identity, then we open ourselves to receiving what we need to know and learn. *Seeing is believing.*

Love, self-esteem, faith, all are important for human life. With these qualities

270

come tolerance, respect, and acceptance. *For what we are we shall receive.*

If we let our fears become a daily part of our life, we are allowing ourselves be guided by feelings of insecurity.

Insecurity will not allow us to make the decisions and changes in our lives that are necessary to us. *Seeing is believing.*

Our daily life is full of surprises, disappointments, full of good or bad things.

When we are insecure, it is very hard to believe in ourselves, and we prefer to stick to something that we know is there, good or bad, instead of cultivating a new attitude that will allow the whole situation to be changed.

In consequence, we deny our fears and put the blame on something or somebody else, because our own insecurity doesn't let us face the reality that we are living. What a waste of time!

Selecting the way we wish to live is up to us. When we make a decision about how we will live our lives, rich or poor, with titles or without them, it will always be our own choice.

You may think that it is impossible, because in some societies people have few choices.

This may sometimes be true, but it is very important to remember that personal efforts are always important, and that we as human beings always make certain choices. We are the only ones who can decide what we really want to be.

We have been talking about material things and social position. But what of being happy or unhappy? This will be our choice, our own decision. It cannot be otherwise.

All we really own is our self, and whatever we decide for us, good or bad, will be our own choice. *Seeing is believing.*

One might say: But sometimes we are motivated by other people's behavior to establish our happiness or unhappiness.

To this one can say that we have the power to stop all kinds of manipulative behavior coming from others.

Mind-power is so extensive that often we can stop things that are making us feel miserable and unhappy.

Self-assurance, awareness, and love for ourselves are the tools that will help us find solutions to these matters. *For what we are we shall receive.*

We see that the life-style that we are living right now is not satisfying us, but we do nothing to stop or to change it.

Why? Because of our desire to have a life that is familiar to us. A life full of mistakes, but we continue living it anyway. *Seeing is believing.*

Why is it so difficult for us to correct

272

ourselves, to get off a path that we have created through errors, but no longer want?

Because change means to us a new belief, a new search, a new beginning, and we are not ready for this. We become paralyzed by the mere idea of change.

Like little children, routines make us feel secure, and any change causes us to fear pain, sacrifice, doubt, insecurity. As human beings already full of problems, we cannot deal with more problems. What a waste of life!

How intricately man, in his fears and ignorance, programs his own life. *Seeing is believing.*

Everything changes with the seasons, except man's mind at times!

In preparation for the times to come, when we need to be ready to renounce the material excesses that we know, will come the renunciation of our familiar life style and acceptance of many kinds of changes.

Changes will imply the necessity of giving love, forgiveness, and sharing.

A life that has no meaning is like being without the sun's light or without the beauty of the seasons.

These are the sensations that connect us with the rest of the Universe.

Everything sounds a little complicated, but if we give to these things the importance they deserve, it will be as simple as drinking a glass of water and tasting it fully.

When we dedicate ourselves a little time to think about these messages with all our heart, we will find that the rewards for doing so will be so precious, that we will run out of the right words to describe them.

The meaning of this message is open to all who can or wish to believe in the possibility of change.

ACKNOWLEDGMENTS

I am very grateful to Eugene S. Urbain and Anabell Aragon for their editorial labors, encouragement and suggestions over the manuscript.

I would like also to deeply express my thanks to my sister Leonor Urbain, Fred Holzapfel and Carl S. Ewert, who have helped me to make this book possible.

AUTHOR'S NOTE

*T*he title of this book was presented to me in a dream, along with the meaning of the word "GEDO", as "In Search of The Light of God". Thus it was explained to me...

ORDER FORM

Mail to : Simu Productions, Inc.
            P.O. Box 6045
            Minneapolis, MN 55406

Qty	Title	Price	Total
	In Search of Gedo	16.95	

Subtotal	
Shipping/handling	5.00
Total	

Name:_____

Address:_____

City, State, Zip_____

Send check or money order (no cash or
COD, please) to Simu Productions, Inc.
Thank you.